A Newfoundland CHRISTMAS

To Laura,
Merry Christmas 2018!
Dawn Baker

A Newfoundland CHRISTMAS

written and illustrated by
Dawn Baker

Note: Any words or phrases that are in ***bold italics*** throughout the book may be found in the glossary in the back.

Pennywell Books
St. John's, NL
2011

Library and Archives Canada Cataloguing in Publication

Baker, Dawn, 1962-
A Newfoundland Christmas / words and pictures by Dawn Baker.

ISBN 978-1-926881-45-4

I. Title.

PS8603.A453N48 2011 jC813'.6 C2011-905199-0

PRINTED IN CANADA

MIX
Paper from responsible sources
FSC
www.fsc.org
FSC® C016245

This paper has been certified to meet the environmental and social standards of the Forest Stewardship Council® (FSC®) and comes from responsibly managed forests, and verified recycled sources.

Pennywell Books is an imprint of Flanker Press Limited.

FLANKER PRESS
P.O. Box 2522, Station C
St. John's, NL A1C 6K1 Canada
TOLL-FREE: 1-866-739-4420
WWW.FLANKERPRESS.COM

10 9 8 7 6 5

Canada

Canada Council for the Arts Conseil des Arts du Canada

Newfoundland Labrador

We acknowledge the [financial] support of the Government of Canada. *Nous reconnaissons l'appui [financier] du gouvernement du Canada.* We acknowledge the support of the Canada Council for the Arts, which last year invested $153 million to bring the arts to Canadians throughout the country. *Nous remercions le Conseil des arts du Canada de son soutien. L'an dernier, le Conseil a investi 153 millions de dollars pour mettre de l'art dans la vie des Canadiennes et des Canadiens de tout le pays.* We acknowledge the financial support of the Government of Newfoundland and Labrador, Department of Tourism, Culture and Recreation for our publishing activities.

In loving memory of my grandparents,
Meta and Arthur Brown
and
Rosie and David Marsh

It was the last day of school before Christmas, but Sarah was not very happy. In fact, she was upset and a little angry. That morning, her mom had told her that they were all going ***down home*** for the holidays. Her older brother, Michael, hadn't seemed very happy about it either.

"This is so unfair!" moaned Sarah to her best friend.

A few days later, Sarah and her family arrived at the home of her nan and pop. As Sarah stepped into the ***saltbox house***, she could smell cinnamon and ginger. Nan's eyes filled with happy tears as she hugged Sarah and Michael, and Pop grinned widely.

"I'm way behind in my Christmas baking," fussed Nan, "but the ***lassy bread*** is still warm if you'd like some, and the ***toutons*** will be ready soon."

Sarah and Michael agreed that the warm, spicy bread full of plump raisins was the best thing that they had ever tasted.

The next morning, Pop woke them a little early.

"Get up, you two ***scallywags***!" he bellowed. "We've got a Christmas tree to get."

They didn't go to a mall or even a Christmas tree lot. Instead, they strapped on snowshoes and stomped into the wooded area outside of the little ***outport*** where Nan and Pop lived. Pop let Sarah pick her favourite tree, and he chopped it down with skill and ease. Michael helped to pull it home.

That evening, Sarah and Michael helped Nan to decorate the tree. It filled the cozy home with the scents of the forest. As they were working, Michael heard something outside. It was music!

When they looked through the window, they saw a Salvation Army Band. It was playing "Silent Night."

Pop went to the door and put some money into the kettle. The music drifted in and around the bay for quite a long time.

Finally, it was Christmas Eve. A great number of aunts, uncles, and cousins had come and gone. There were many tempting gifts under the tree, although Santa had yet to arrive.

Nan coaxed everyone into their Sunday best for the late-night service. The church bell rang out bright and clear through the frosty air. Snow began to fall.

Christmas morning was loud and fun! Christmas dinner was tasty! Besides turkey and dressing, they ate ***salt beef*** and vegetables, ***pease pudding*** and gravy, and ***figgy duff***.

After their wonderful meal, Sarah and Michael joined some of their cousins and new friends. They went sliding down Uncle Dave's hill. Sarah's new sled and Dad's old coaster took turns flying down the hill.

A day later, Sarah watched as the snow melted from her ***double-ball mitts***. Drops of water dripped down and sizzled on the woodstove. She thought about earlier that day when they had gone for a sleigh ride.

The sleigh had been pulled along by Buddy. He was Aunt Elizabeth's ***Newfoundland Pony***. Buddy was almost as white as the snow, and Sarah thought he was the most beautiful animal she had ever seen.

A loud knocking startled Sarah out of her daydream.

"Any ***mummers*** 'lowed in?" many voices shouted, as a fantastic assortment of merrymakers burst through the door.

There was laughing and dancing and singing and eating and teasing and guessing! Michael took a turn on the ***ugly stick***, and Pop played the ***button accordion***.

Most of the next morning was slept away. Nan told them they were all at risk of becoming ***hangashores***! However, her eyes were twinkling as she said it.

That afternoon, Michael joined in on a spirited game of scrap hockey. He was considered by all to be one of the stars. No one was quite sure which side scored the most goals, but it was easy to declare the winners – everyone!

Time passed so quickly that Sarah found herself back home and back at school before she knew it. Her best friend was very happy to see her.

"How was your Newfoundland Christmas?" asked her friend. "Was it as awful as you thought it would be?"

Sarah just smiled and replied, "All I can say is that I sure hope we can go ***down home*** for Christmas again next year!"

DB

Glossary

Button accordion is a type of accordion on which the melody-side keyboard has buttons rather than keys. It has long been a traditional instrument of Newfoundland.

Double-ball mitts are hand-knit mittens that are created by knitting with two balls of different coloured wool at the same time. They feature intricate and beautiful patterns.

Down home is a phrase that, when used by Newfoundlanders, frequently refers to returning to the island, often from mainland Canada.

Figgy duff is a traditional Newfoundland sweet pudding with raisins. It is usually boiled in a cotton bag in a large pot along with salt beef and root vegetables.

Hangashore is a term that once referred to a man who was too lazy to fish for a living. Now it refers to anyone who is considered lazy.

Lassy bread is a beloved spice-molasses bread full of raisins. It is also known as sweet bread in some areas of Newfoundland and Labrador.

Mummers are holiday visitors that arrive in disguise around Christmastime. The hosts have to try to guess the identities of the visitors. Mummering has been a part of Newfoundland and Labrador holidays for centuries. In recent years, there has been a mummering revival.

Newfoundland Pony is a breed of pony whose ancestors are from the British Isles. It is handsome, strong, and hard-working – like most Newfoundlanders! In 1997, the Newfoundland Pony was recognized by the Government of Newfoundland and Labrador as the province's first heritage animal.

Outports are small, sometimes isolated, coastal communities in Newfoundland and Labrador. They are some of the oldest European settlements in Canada.

Pease pudding is a savoury pudding created with dried split yellow peas, salt, and pepper. It is considered by many to be an essential part of Jiggs' dinner.

Salt beef is a food staple in nearly every kitchen in Newfoundland and Labrador. It is beef that has been preserved by salt-curing and, like pease pudding, it is a requirement for Jiggs' dinner.

Saltbox house is a wooden-frame house with a long, pitched roof that slopes down lower in the back (similar in shape to a once-common box for salt). It also features a flat front and a central chimney. At one time, it was a very popular house design in Newfoundland outports, and it is now enjoying a return to popularity in the province.

Scallywag is a word that means rascal. In Newfoundland, it is sometimes used as a term of endearment, especially when used by an older person speaking to a child.

Toutons are similar to pancakes. They are created by pan-frying white bread dough that has risen. Toutons are usually served with butter and molasses.

Ugly stick refers to a traditional mummering instrument. It is often made of a mop or broom handle with bottle caps loosely nailed into it. An ugly stick is played by tapping it on the floor or by using another stick to rattle the bottle caps.

Dawn Baker is a writer and artist living in Gander, Newfoundland and Labrador. Her career as an artist began when she was very young because she loved to draw and paint and was encouraged to do so. She grew up in Glenwood, in central Newfoundland, and moved to Gander as a teenager. In 1992, she had her first one-woman exhibition, and in 1995, she created her own Art Works Studio in Gander.

Dawn has a bachelor of education (post secondary) and a certificate in library studies, both from Memorial University. She has been a board member of The Rooms Corporation of Newfoundland and Labrador since 2006, and she is the current chair of its education and lifelong learning committee.